I0765531

MURF

THE MASTER SURF BLASTER

DALE BAKER

A local Legend lives in our town, who everyone knows from all around.

A little baby elephant who loves to surf! No-one quite like our little mate Murf.

He blasts over the waves with style and ease, performing tricks on his head and knees.

Doing flips in the air while giving a smile, he's the best thing in town by a country mile.

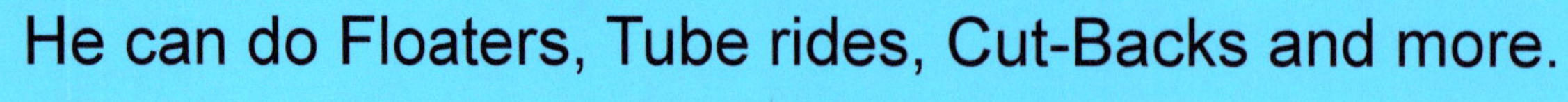

He can do Floaters, Tube rides, Cut-Backs and more.

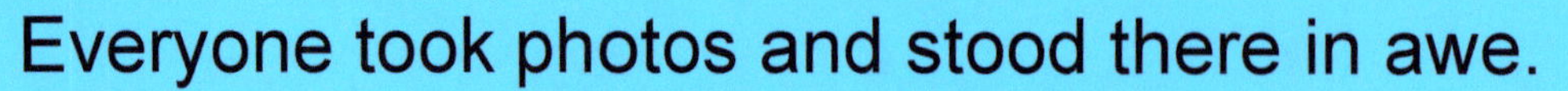

Everyone took photos and stood there in awe.

Across the internet and news, our little mate was there.

Murf the little elephant, surfed with grace and flair.

Murf eventually went viral, and was on a complete roll!
But slowly his confidence sunk and spiraled out of control.

Crowds used to line the beaches just to get a glimpse,
 but things changed a lot for our poor Murf since .

As his body grew bigger and bigger, he found it harder and harder to surf.

This was the beginning of the end for 'The surfing career of Murf'.

Surfing was his identity, it was all he knew.

Murf started to ponder, what was he going to do?

He chewed over possible jobs but really was quite stuck.

He thought 'Maybe I'll fight fires on the back of a fire truck?'

But carrying Murph around wasn't helpful for the brigade.

Their truck just couldn't handle how much poor Murph weighed.

He tried giving tourist joyrides in the town a go.
But this didn't last long as Murf was just too slow.

He tried painting pictures of others with his huge trunk.
But this didn't last either, as his painting always stunk.

He tried everything he could think of, but it all appeared in vain.
If it wasn't to do with surfing, it just wasn't quite the same.

Sadly, Murf found himself in a dark slump and grew slightly depressed.

'I'll never find the right job for me' he sighed, becoming quite distressed.

Murf scrolled through his old surf photos, 'Ah-Ha! That's it!'
'I could be a surf photographer, that's the perfect fit!'

He was stoked to get the back in the water and take pics of the waves,
and knew the big Surf Comp was approaching in several days.

Surfing

Elephants are great swimmers and Murf's camera was waterproof.

He took excellent photos, and his sales went through the roof.

And on the days with no waves no-one was bored or worried like in the past.

As Murf would jump from the diving board, to give the waves a

Yep! A local Legend lives in our town, who everyone knows from all around.

A big friendly elephant who loves to photograph the surf.

There's no-one quite like, our big mate Murf.

OTHER GREAT BOOKS BY DALE BAKER

Arty Farty Marty, the paint smashin' kraken

How to be Clever Forever

Flip

The World's #1 Talking Bum
(Graphic Novel)

Dream a Dream

The Surf Dogs, A Whale's Tale

How to Be an Artist

Bobby Dazzla, Torquay Time Traveller
(Graphic Novel)

9 780645 815511